DISCARDED

The Real Princess

To my husband Mike for all his love and encouragement, and
for my children, Susie and Jonathan, whose childhood so delighted
me it has been my inspiration ever since. With love — B. W.

To my dear friend Aline — S. F.

Barefoot Books
2067 Massachusetts Ave
Cambridge, MA 02140

Text copyright © 2008 by Brenda Williams
Illustrations copyright © 2008 by Sophie Fatus
The moral right of Brenda Williams to be identified as
the author and Sophie Fatus to be identified as
the illustrator of this work has been asserted

This book has been printed on 100% acid-free paper

Graphic design by Louise Millar, London
Color separation by Grafiscan, Verona
Printed and bound in Singapore by Tien Wah Press

This book was typeset in Meridien and Girls Are Weird
The illustrations were prepared in acrylics with collaged papers

Library of Congress Cataloging-in-Publication Data
Williams, Brenda.
The real princess / Brenda Williams.
   p. cm.
Summary: A queen devises a way, with the help of her nine golden peas, to tell
whether each of the girls her three sons hope to marry is a true princess.
ISBN-13: 978-1-905236-88-6
[1. Fairy tales. 2. Kings, queens, rulers, etc.--Fiction. 3. Princesses--Fiction.] I. Title.

PZ8.W66923Rea 2006
[E]--dc22

2005032530
1 3 5 7 9 8 6 4 2

The Real Princess

A Mathemagical Tale

written by Brenda Williams

illustrated by Sophie Fatus

Barefoot Books
Celebrating Art and Story

Long ago and far away, a king and queen had 3 sons. The eldest son was named Primo and the second son was named Secundo. The third son was named Terzo.

The king and queen had
1 butler, 2 footmen,
3 maids, 4 horses,
5 grooms, 6 dogs,
7 gardeners, 8 chimney sweeps,
9 cooks and
10 soldiers.

Now, the king had a counting house in which he kept 3 bags of gold. Each bag contained 180 gold coins.

"One day my sons will marry,"
the king said to himself.
"These bags of gold will give
them a fine start in life."

Now, it was the custom at that time that the eldest prince should marry first, but only if he could find a bride fit to be the next queen.

"You must find yourself a *real* princess," said his father every morning as he dug into his royal breakfast. "Only a *real* princess will do."

So Primo set off to find a wife. He searched far and wide, but he found fault with every princess he met. "Her nose is too pointy, and she's much too bossy to be a *real* princess," he sighed. "Her feet are too floppity, and she won't look me in the eye," he complained. The truth was, he simply could not tell if a girl was a *real* princess or not.

Primo returned home full of gloom. "I wish so much to marry a *real* princess, mother," he sighed, "but how can I tell if she's *real* or not?"

"Leave it to me," said the queen. "I have a test that will prove beyond a doubt whether she is a *real* princess or not."

Now you may like to know what no one else in the castle knew. The queen too had a counting house. It was a small, shabby shed hidden away at the back of the gooseberry patch, and in it she kept 9 golden peas.

When the queen opened the door of the shed, the peas gleamed in the darkness. The queen smiled as she counted them, for she knew a secret about the peas.

The next day, a terrible storm came. It was
so wet and wild that the 10 soldiers and the
7 gardeners had to abandon their duties and
come inside for shelter.

Then, just as the storm was at its worst,
Terzo heard someone knocking frantically
— *knock! knock! knock!* —
on the castle door.

Standing outside was a young girl, and she
was in a sorry state. The rain had drenched
her clothing right through, and her hair fell
in dripping straggles down to her waist.
But as soon as their eyes met, Terzo's heart
skipped a beat, and there was a spring in
his step as he ushered her inside.

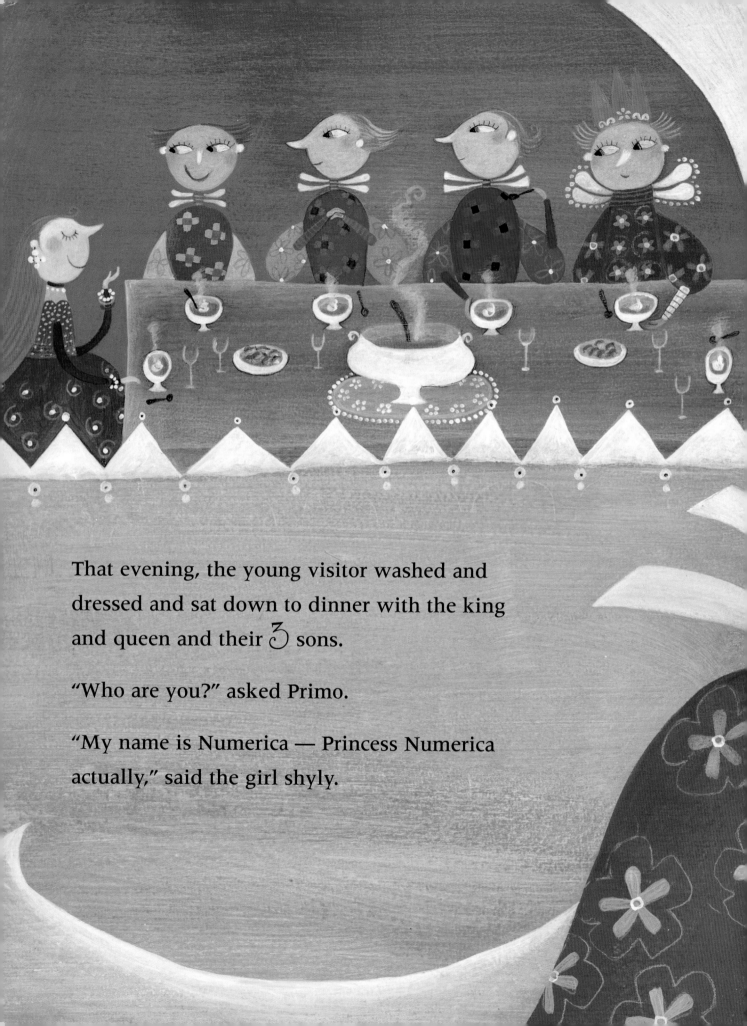

That evening, the young visitor washed and dressed and sat down to dinner with the king and queen and their 3 sons.

"Who are you?" asked Primo.

"My name is Numerica — Princess Numerica actually," said the girl shyly.

The queen studied her through narrowed eyes.
Then, while everyone else ate lobster soup made
by the 9 palace cooks, she slipped away to prepare
a bed. She asked her 3 maids to bring up 6 mattresses
and 7 feather beds from the linen room.
When the bed was ready, the queen
tucked 5 golden peas under
the bottom mattress.

The next morning at breakfast, the queen inquired of the girl: "How did you sleep, my dear?"

"Oh, wonderfully, thank you," her guest replied. "I did not wake until I heard the cockerel crow."

The queen shook her head slowly. Then she went to the bedroom and threw the 5 peas out of the window.

But Terzo was delighted.

"She is princess enough for me," he said. "I love her just the way she is."

So the king took Terzo to his counting house and gave 1 of the bags of gold to his youngest son.

The young prince and the princess, who was not quite a *real* princess, married and lived happily ever after.

Now when the king went to his counting house,
he counted only 2 bags of gold.

And when the queen went to her counting house,
she had only 4 golden peas to count.

One day, a dense, damp fog came down over the
kingdom. The castle was hidden in a swirling, grey
mist, and the paths seemed to merge into the bushes.

Just when the fog was at its thickest, there was a
loud knocking — *knock! knock! knock!* — on
the castle door. This time, Secundo went to open it.
Standing outside was a young girl, and she was in a
sorry state. Her dress had been torn to shreds by brambles.
Her arms were cut and scratched and bruised, and her hair
was tangled and matted with leaves and burrs. But as soon
as he set eyes on her, Secundo felt his heart turn a somersault.

That evening, the young visitor washed and dressed and tended to her cuts and bruises. Then she sat down to dinner with the king and queen and their 2 sons.

"Who are you?" asked Primo.

"I am Princess Calcula," replied the girl in a rather grand voice. "My parents live in a palace that is twice this size, and they have 3 times as many servants."

The queen looked at her guest carefully. She thought they might at last have found a *real* princess, for the girl had been brave about her injuries, and she appeared to be very well off.

While Princess Calcula told everyone about her family's many servants, the queen slipped away to prepare a bed. This time, her 3 maids brought up 8 mattresses and 9 feather beds from the linen room, and the queen tucked 3 golden peas beneath the bottom mattress.

The next morning at breakfast, the queen inquired of the girl: "How did you sleep, my dear?"

"Oh, wonderfully, thank you," her guest replied. "I did not wake until I heard the cockerel crow."

The queen shook her head slowly. And she went to the bedroom and threw the 3 golden peas out of the window.

But Secundo was delighted. "She is princess enough for me," he said. "I love her just the way she is."

So the king took Secundo to his counting house and gave 1 of the 2 remaining bags of gold to his son.

The young prince and the princess, who was not quite a *real* princess — but very nearly a *real* princess — married and lived happily ever after.

Now when the king went to his counting house, he counted only 1 bag of gold.

And when the queen went to her counting house, she only had 1 golden pea left.

That summer, a heat wave descended upon the kingdom. The wide, rushing river sparkled as it flowed through the valley. Butterflies danced in the sunlight and flowers opened their petals wide.

Primo was riding back to the castle after another failed journey to find a *real* princess when he heard someone singing. There, sitting in the shade of a tall oak tree, was a young girl. She was weaving flowers into a garland for her hair. She smiled at the prince and wished him a safe journey.

But Primo had no intention of going a step further. He quickly dismounted and tied up his horse.

"Who are you?" he asked.

"Hmm. Let me see. Today, my name's Geometria," she said. "What's yours?"

"Primo. Prince Primo, as a matter of fact. Errr . . . are you a princess, by any chance?"

The girl raised her left eyebrow and looked him straight in the eye.

"You'll have to judge that for yourself," she said. "Why don't you stop asking questions and come exploring instead?"

So the 2 of them wandered the woods together, watching the doves and butterflies come and go and talking of many things. When evening fell, they rode back to the castle together.

That night, the young visitor washed and dressed and sat down to dinner with the king and queen and their 1 son.

"Thank you so much for inviting me to stay," she said, with a voice that rang like silver bells. "I hope you will all come and visit my family one day soon."

The queen smiled as she listened. She only wanted the best for her son, and their visitor was enchanting. But was she a princess? While the rest of the party ate their ice cream sundaes, which had been created from a secret recipe by the 9 palace cooks, the queen slipped away to prepare a bed. This time, her 3 maids brought up 9 mattresses and 10 feather beds from the linen room. And this time, the queen tucked just 1 golden pea beneath the bottom mattress.

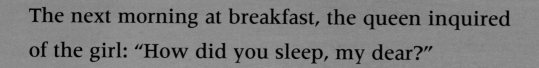

The next morning at breakfast, the queen inquired
of the girl: "How did you sleep, my dear?"

"Oh, I'm sorry to complain, when you have been so kind to
me," her guest said, "but although I had 9 mattresses, and
10 feather beds, I felt most uncomfortable all night, and I am
black-and-blue all over."

The queen looked at her eldest son and smiled. "Then she must indeed be a *real* princess, my son," she said, "for only a real princess would feel just 1 golden pea through 9 mattresses and 10 feather beds. You have found your true love at last!"

And she went to the bedroom, and threw the pea out of the window.

So the king took his eldest son to his counting house and gave him the last bag of gold.

And the queen went to her counting house, but of course she had no peas left. For though she had once had 9 peas, she had used 5 peas for the first girl, 3 peas for the second girl, and 1 pea for the third girl, and each time she had flung them out of the window!

But the queen smiled, for she knew a secret about the peas.

The prince and the princess, who truly was a *real* princess and would one day be queen, married and lived happily ever after.

The End — almost.

(but not quite.)

Actually, that is not quite the end of the story. For now the king had no money left in his counting house as he had given it all to his sons.

That night, he asked the queen, "How shall we manage, my dear? We have so many faithful servants who look after us — how shall we feed and pay them?"

"Come with me," said the queen.

So the king followed the queen into the garden.

There, beneath the bedroom window, the 9 golden peas had each taken root, and grown into 9 tall plants. But on just 1 of the plants shone lots of golden pea pods.

"This is from the pea that Princess Geometria slept on," smiled the queen. "That young woman is worth her weight in gold, mark my words."

She picked a pod, and inside it glowed 9 golden
peas. She picked another pod, and found 9 more.
Then she picked 7 more pods, and handed them to
the king.

"My dear," she said softly, "I think we have quite
enough for our needs."

The king was astonished and flabbergasted and speechless with delight. He hugged the queen and danced her all around the castle grounds.

And the 1 butler, 2 footmen, 3 maids,
4 horses, 5 grooms, 6 dogs, 7 gardeners,
8 chimney sweeps, 9 cooks and 10 soldiers
all joined in the dancing.

The Real End!

TEST YOUR COUNTING SKILLS!

- How many windows can you count on the castle?

- How many gold coins does each of the king's bags contain?

- How many gold coins does the king have altogether?

- How many gold coins does the king have after he has given one bag to Terzo?

- How many animals live in the castle?

- How many servants live in the castle?

- How many servants does Princess Calcula's family employ?

- If there are 9 golden peas in each pod, how many golden peas will the king and queen have when they have opened all 9 pods?

- 9 is a rather magical number, because it always adds up to itself. Whatever number you multiply 9 by, you will find that the numerals add up to 9 — try it and see!

To find the answers to these questions,
visit www.barefootbooks.com and search for The Real Princess.
GOOD LUCK!

Barefoot Books
Celebrating Art and Story

At Barefoot Books, we celebrate art and story that opens
the hearts and minds of children from all walks of life,
inspiring them to read deeper, search further, and explore
their own creative gifts. Taking our inspiration from many
different cultures, we focus on themes that encourage
independence of spirit, enthusiasm for learning, and sharing
of the world's diversity. Interactive, playful and beautiful,
our products combine the best of the present with the
best of the past to educate our children
as the caretakers of tomorrow.

Live Barefoot!

Join us at www.barefootbooks.com